LISA VAN DER WIELEN

DEAR UNIVERSE

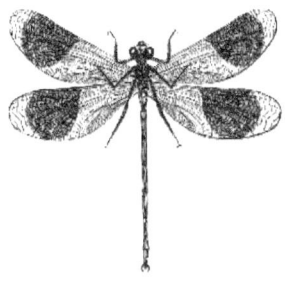

DEAR UNIVERSE

For Matt

My universe within the universe.

By

Lisa Van Der Wielen

First Printed 2023

ISBN: 9780645397949 (Paperback)

ISBN: 9780645397956 (Hardback)

Cover and text design by Lisa Van Der Wielen

Set in Times New Roman

www.lisavanderwielen.com

Contents

The universe is a very strange thing. Just when we think we have it all figured out, something happens to question our beliefs once again. Funny thing is, sometimes we are so caught up in our own little universe, we are unaware of the connections around us. But with time, the power of the universe and these connections present themselves through intertwining paths and subtle signs. This is a story about the power of the universe, but most importantly, the power of belief in oneself.

1

Elise

11th January 1996

Dear Universe,

My name is Elise. I am nearly sixteen years old. I love playing sport; swimming is the absolute best! I have been a swimmer most of my life, and being in the water is my happy place. I love school and learning, but I'm not even sure what I want to be yet. My teachers suggest I should study medicine or law, but I'm not so certain, it's too hard to choose one path.

I've never had a boyfriend, but I'd really like one. I have lots of friends that are boys, but not boyfriends. Sometimes boys are so much easier to get along with than girls. I'm not in the popular group, but I'm not in the geek group either -in fact, I don't really even have a specific group, but I still have lots of friends. I'm the studious type, so apparently that means I'm not super-cool and often makes me a target for bullies - well it certainly did at my old school. I have to hide my braininess as people find it intimidating and you only get teased for it. I tend to just ignore them as I know it's a reflection on them, not me, but sometimes it does get to me. I can't help but believe what they are saying about me at times.

All the boys at my school are boring and so immature, so I've never felt that crazy crush feeling all my girlfriends talk about. That is until now. Today I met the most amazing guy - as soon as I saw him I felt the butterflies in my stomach. It was as if my whole body and soul knew this person was going to be a significant person in my life. Crazy I know, but it was like you were trying to tell me something, Universe!

My best friend Hannah had convinced me to come to Summer Sailing Camp with her. I figured ten days on the beach sounds perfect to me, swimming and being on the water is my kind of fun! I didn't know anyone else going, only Hannah, but hopefully I'd make new friends. The moment we arrived this morning and walked down to the beach, I glanced over at a group of young men sitting on the sand. They were laughing and joking around as they do. As I walked down the sandy, wooden steps leading the shoreline, I met eyes with one of them and he smiled.

I whispered to Hannah, "Who is that guy?"

She replied, "Oh that's Steven Thompson, all the girls like him. He's a volleyball player and surfs and plays guitar in a band. So, join the queue, you've got no chance!"

Just as I felt the disappointment of her comments run through me, he looked over at me once again and grinned. I felt those butterflies once more. Even though I knew what she was saying is probably true and I'd have no chance with a guy like that, I couldn't help but be intrigued by him. He seemed different to any other guys I've met. He has a kindness behind his eyes and that genuine presence that I can almost feel touching my soul. I can sense he views the world a little differently, just like myself.

So please, Universe, can you help a girl out here? I better get my beauty sleep now as tomorrow is the first day of sailing, I have absolutely no idea what to do but I'll learn. I hope I get to be on the boat with him!!

Sweet dreams Universe, goodnight.

Elise xx

12th January 1996

Dear Universe,

Thank you! Thank you! Thank you! It must have worked. I asked you to help me out and you did. I got to be on his boat today. I couldn't believe it! When I woke up this morning, instead of going straight to the hall for breakfast, I crept down to the boat shed to check the rosters for the day. My heart started beating faster when I saw the words, 'Catamaran 21, Steven and Elise.' I tried to wipe the smile off my face so others wouldn't notice, but it was a bit difficult to hide.

I heard the girls talking about which boat they wanted to be on as they walked back from breakfast.
"How did *she* get to be on Steven's boat?" one asked.
"It must be because she is new or something." I heard another reply.
I tried not to let the insecurities creep in, but it can be a bit hard dealing with teenage girls sometimes, especially when you've grown up with brothers. I just don't get how mean and competitive girls can be. Shouldn't we be building each other up, not trying to bring each other down?

I started stressing when I went back to the dorm about which bathers I should wear, and whether I should wear my hair tied up or leave it out. I didn't want to put too much sunscreen on my face to look like a ghost (although now I wish I'd used a little more as I got a bit sunburned)). I don't wear makeup like the other girls. I just don't see the point with watersports, as wearing mascara soon has you looking like a panda bear!

When it was time to set sail for the first time, I felt the butterflies in my stomach again. It was like I was standing on the swimming blocks ready for a race, the same kind of nerves but a bit different. As soon as we both hopped on the boat though, I started to relax more. Steven made me feel at ease, he was so lovely, showed me what to do and before we knew it, we were sailing across the turquoise-blue water. We chatted nonstop the whole time, about school and our love for sport and music. I didn't want that time to end. It was like seconds stood still and it was just the two of us out on the water, forgetting about all the other boats out there. Towards the end of our sail, I felt him sitting closer to me and every now and then he would glance over and smile at me. We laughed and found ourselves just chatting about life in general. When he smiles, his eyes smile too. His eyes were the colour of the water and as the sunlight played on his suntan, I could see the cute, faint little freckles across his nose. I could feel these gushes of emotions sweep over me every time he looked at me and grinned.

When our boat glided ashore, I felt disappointed that our alone time together had come to an end. As we walked to the boat shed together to return our safety vests, I thanked him for making my first sailing experience so enjoyable.

"I had a great time, hopefully we can do it again," he said.

I smiled and agreed. Hopefully, that means something, Universe!

As soon as I returned to camp to shower, all the girls were asking me *how it was* and *what did he say?* I didn't want to give too much information away and I didn't want them to know I really liked him, so I just replied with a brief, "yeah, it was good."

Then it dawned on me, Universe - I really like this guy. What if he doesn't feel the same way? Like I think he does, I sense he does, but what if I'm wrong? I'm just going to get hurt. Anyway, it was a great day.

I headed back to the dorm. Steven's older sister is head of my dormitory, and she is sleeping on my bottom bunk. What if she finds out I like her brother? She might not even like me. Hannah is in a different dorm, and I don't know the other girls. I can tell by the way they look at me that they don't want me to fit in here. And maybe it's just me being oversensitive as usual, but I feel like I don't really fit in here, either.

Elise xx

13th January 1996

Dear Universe,

I didn't get to see Steven much today. I was on a different boat. He probably got to sail with a much prettier girl today and he won't even remember who I am. I think my friend Hannah likes him too. Maybe that is why she wasn't very encouraging when I was asking about him. I am not even missing home that much like I thought I would, I guess because we are so busy each day. Although I do miss my dog and having a nice bath! There are only showers here and you only get three minutes under the warm water and then you get kicked out! How on earth is a girl supposed to shave her legs in that time, let alone wash her hair! There is only one mirror in the shower block, so I'm lucky if I can even catch a glimpse of my reflection in the background behind the skinny, popular girls who hog the mirror each day.

Tomorrow night there is a Bush Dance and games night. I'd better wear something to cover the massive bruise I got on my leg today from flying into the boom of the boat - the guy I was sailing with had absolutely no idea and the boat was going all over the place. It didn't help that I was wishing I was with Steven the whole time and not paying much attention to what I was doing. Please Universe, don't let me get any big pimples on my face when I wake up in the morning, I want to be looking my best tomorrow.

Goodnight world.

Elise xx

14th January 1996

Dear Universe,

Tonight was so much fun! We dressed up like country bumpkins and bootscooted through the sand dunes to country music. We played a cool version of hide-and-seek in the dark with torches. I was a bit worried about being in the bushland at night with all the creepy crawlies as I am always the first person to get bitten by insects. There were huge spider webs everywhere, you could see them glistening in the torch beams. I was nervous, as I hoped tonight would be the night that Steven actually kissed me, but the universe had other plans!

At one point, he and I were hiding behind a shrub. He put his arm around me as we bobbed down hiding from the others. I felt tingles all over as his hand touched my back. I could just make out his face in the moonlight and feel his gaze beholding me. Our faces were so close; I could feel him breathing against my cheek. I knew as soon as I looked into his eyes that our lips would become closer. I was afraid to look up, as I had never kissed anyone before, even though more than anything I wanted to feel his lips on mine. As I glanced up into his eyes and felt Steven move closer, I worried that he could feel my heart racing through my chest. Thoughts ran through my head, I couldn't believe that this moment had finally arrived. Unfortunately though, the blissful moment of expectation was rudely interrupted as we were suddenly blinded by the glare of a torch beam. We stood there staring like deer in the headlights. We had been caught! We headed back to base, our romantic moment spoiled. A moment I hope we will have the opportunity for once again!

Elise xx

21st January 1996

Dear Universe,

Well, it is time to say goodbye to Sailing Camp tomorrow. I can't believe how quickly the past ten days have gone. I am looking forward to getting home to my own comfy bed - I don't think I will miss snoozing in a sleeping bag on the top bunk. But I also don't want life to go back to reality. As much as I miss my family and home, I don't want this summer to end.

Everyone went for a beach walk tonight, being our last night here. I felt the sadness wash over me like the small waves washed over our toes. I wasn't going to let that sadness ruin my last night here, though. The last night spent with Steven and all the other girls vying for his attention! I knew tonight was going to be our last chance to get some alone time before everyone leaves in the morning. Hannah and the girls were wanting me to walk with them, but every now and then Steven would walk up beside me. We would start chatting and find ourselves at the back of the line in our own little world. As we were strolling along the water's edge, I felt his hand brush up against mine, as though he wanted to grab it. It felt like the whole world was watching and we would become the talk of the group, but once again our moment was spoiled by fellow campers wanting us to join them.

I just wanted to sit with him on the beach, to be alone and to talk. I wanted him to hold me in his athletic arms and kiss me like he was going to last night. As we were heading back to the dorms to go to bed, Steven came to the veranda to say goodnight. He smiled at me with the cute little smile lines around his eyes and said, "I'll catch the bus home to the city with you tomorrow, as there is something I want to ask you."

I could feel my heart start beating faster with excitement once again, but I had to play it cool on the outside, so I just replied with, "Okay, sounds good, see you tomorrow then, good night!"

PLEASE UNIVERSE, help me get Steven to ask me to be his girlfriend tomorrow! I have no idea how I am going to fall asleep tonight, I am so excited.

Sweet dreams, Universe!

Elise xx

22nd January 1996

Dear Universe,

I sit here on the bus, looking out the window. I don't want the others to see the disappointment and sadness on my face, so I still smile, but that smile is just a facade for what I really feel underneath. Why didn't Steven come on the bus home with me like he promised? Am I not pretty enough? Skinny enough? Smart enough? Maybe he thinks I am too young for him; he is getting his licence next week and I am not even sixteen yet. Maybe it's because I'm not part of the popular group? Maybe it's because I'm not part of the church group and his family don't approve? I thought he liked me, I thought he actually really liked me as much as I like him. I thought we had a real connection, like nothing I have ever felt before. A connection as deep and meaningful as the universe! I guess I was wrong.

Goodbye Sailing Camp, lot of memories and connections made, but that chapter is closed now. I will probably never see Steven again and that makes me feel sad. I just don't get it, what is it with me and boys? I always seem to scare them away somehow. I am never going to get a boyfriend! I think I am going to sign out from all of this universe business for a while. Sorry to say it, but I don't think it really works - I mean asking the universe for things seems a little ridiculous, doesn't it? Like destiny and fate, what's meant to be, will be. Is it really written in the stars? I don't know, Universe, I really don't know anymore. I am starting to think we are the creators of our own destiny.

Elise xx

2
Steven

11th January 1996

Dear Universe,

My name is Steven Thompson, but my mates call me
Tommo. I'm turning seventeen in a couple of weeks,
so I will be going for my driver's licence. I haven't
told anyone that I'm nervous about it and I'm worried
I'll fail, so you might have to help me out a bit,
Universe! All my friends are counting on me to get my
licence so we can go surfing whenever we want.

I'm about to start my final year of high school and I
still don't know what path to choose. I guess I can't
play sport all my life, and music isn't going to get me a
full-time career, so I know I will have to put my head
in the books at some stage. But there's plenty of time
for that. At least we have a couple of weeks on the
beach before I need to worry about school again,
although it's a pity there aren't any waves here in the
bay. But I'm thinking maybe this Summer Sailing
Camp I'm at, the one my family make me go on each

24

year, isn't going to be so bad after all. This cool chic is here, golden blonde hair, tanned skin and cute smile. I really want to hang out with her so I'm going to volunteer to have her on my boat to teach her the sailing ropes. I'm sure they won't even notice me changing the names on the list!

Steven

12th January 1996

Dear Universe,

Great day on the boat with Elise, glad my plan to change the rosters worked, no one even noticed, not even my brother! She is such a cool chick. I am going to try and hang out with her some more. She's smart and funny, not to even mention the contrast of her tanned skin and blonde hair with those mesmerising blue eyes! I wish there were more waves down here so I could show off my surfing skills, but there's not a wave in sight! I'll have to try something else to show off my talents. I might need some help to get some more alone time with her. It's a bit hard with both Mum and Dad and my brother and sister here! I better think of something.

A day spent on the water has made me hungry, can't wait to see what is for dinner! Oh, that's right, Mum is cooking for the camp, so I better not expect a gourmet buffet. I wish my mum was a better cook!

Steven

14th January 1996

Dear Universe,

I had a great night at camp this evening. I got to spend some time alone with Elise, but not long enough! I was just about to kiss her when along came Mark to spoil it all. He was shining his torch in our faces, right when I was ready to pounce. I wanted to deck him one but had to play it cool. Well, there is always tomorrow night! I am nervous about playing guitar in front of her tomorrow night. Wish me luck!

Steven

22nd January 1996

Dear Universe,

She is gone and I didn't even get to say goodbye. I
wanted to catch that bus home today, but my parents
wouldn't let me! They made me stay back to help
clean up the camp. I am not a little kid anymore! I'm
about to get my licence, yet they treat me like I'm still
a five-year-old at times! I am so pissed off right now. I
have checked the camp book and she hasn't even put
her phone number in it. You might have to help me out
Universe. Help me see Elise again!
Steven

3
Hole Hearted

8th March 2012

Dear Universe,

I know it's been a while since I have spoken to you. A long time since I have truly asked something from you.

The white sterile walls of the ward, the beeping of the medical machines and the smell of chlorine and disinfectant are making it difficult for me to sleep. It may also be the daunting thought of what tomorrow's surgery might bring.

Chlorine, the smell of chlorine. The scent of chlorine brings back nostalgic memories for me, from my happy childhood - a time when life was simple. When we see or hear things from our childhood it reminds us of the past, but when we smell something that evokes memories, we feel as though we're back in that moment. The waft of pool chlorine makes me want to dive back in that pool and swim away, leaving the worries behind. My affinity with the water has always been a part of my life, but marriage, work and children have kept me from swimming that black line for many years.

Maybe I will get back into that pool one day, who knows. They say you never forget how to ride a bike or a horse, so I'm sure I haven't forgotten how to stay between the lane ropes! Anyway, life keeps moving us forward, although it's hard to see forward if we are always looking back. I think tomorrow, to keep myself calm, I am going to imagine myself swimming. Just keep swimming Elise, keep swimming. So, can I ask you one favour, Universe? Please keep me swimming. Please help get me through the open-heart surgery tomorrow. I don't want to leave my daughter without a mum. Please Universe, I have so much left to do in this world. I need much more time.

Elise xx

9th March 2012

Dear Universe,

The day has arrived. As I lay here on a white bed, in a white room, writing on white paper, I am hoping this isn't a sign from you that it's time for me to see the 'white light.'

The nurses asked my husband to say goodbye to me as they wheeled me into this sterile room. One of them, petite in stature with a chirpy manner, was trying to make the atmosphere calm and positive. I could sense she was doing her best to create a more positive environment for everyone.

"How about you say goodbye, relax for ten minutes and wait for the pre-meds to take effect, and we will see you very shortly," she said as she grabbed my hand.
I smiled back at her. Ivan didn't say a word. He bent down and kissed me on the forehead like a robot, completely emotionless as he left the room. He didn't ask me how I was feeling, nor if I was okay. He didn't seem to show an ounce of emotion. He would not even make eye contact with me. Cold, cruel and heartless.

He didn't seem affected at all that his wife could now be taking her last breaths. Not a skerrick of emotion on his face.

That is not love. That is not caring for someone. That is not compassion and empathy. I know deep down that man despises me, I guess I just haven't wanted to believe it. I haven't wanted to face what consequences that truth brings. I sense he doesn't want me to make it through the surgery, but I just can't let that happen. I have to fight; I have to make it through this, and I will.

These ten minutes of waiting seem like ten years. This could well be my last journal entry. I don't want to even think about the risk of death or something going wrong, but I can't help but feel the seriousness of what I'm about to face. In just minutes, my heart is going to stop beating and a machine will be pumping blood through my veins. My heart will be taken out of my body to be repaired. The operation will take many arduous hours. I am literally putting my heart into the hands of these surgeons.

All of these years without even realising, I have been walking around with a large hole in my heart. For all that time, I felt like part of my heart was missing when in fact it actually was. I have always felt a bit lost in this world at times. I can't help but reflect on my life and what I have and haven't achieved. How quickly the years have passed. What would I have done differently? What would I change if I could? What really is the most important thing in life? Well, I know the answer to that one - it is *love*. We cannot survive without it. Love brings meaning and purpose to life. I think the hardest thing to face right now is the fact that I no longer have that love from the one person in my life that I should. I see now that I probably never did, and I know I never will.

I lay here, hole-hearted in the hope I will wake up whole-hearted. See you on the other side, Universe.

Elise xx

4

Departed

21st May 2014

Dear Universe,

How can this be happening again? I thought I had conquered this mountain but here I am again in the sterile white walls of a hospital emergency room, listening to the beep of machines and waiting for doctors to decide what action to take. I thought the surgery two years ago had fixed my heart and once I got through it all everything would be okay, but congenital heart disease doesn't work that way. Once a heart patient, always a heart patient.

At least now I am conscious and able to write. I can't remember the whole trip of how I got here, just parts of it as I went in and out of consciousness. I don't know what I would do without my angel of a neighbour and friend Jean, who drove me here quicker than the ambulance could have. They have called my husband, but he is busy at work. I am sure he will get here eventually. My parents are looking after my daughter. Hopefully, the surgery won't keep me in hospital too long this time.

The doctors think I can't hear them talking, but I can hear them chatting about my atrial fibrillation and brachycardia and the need for a pacemaker. Great! It looks like I am getting pacemaker surgery. More chest scars to contend with, but at least it will keep me alive.

Please, Universe, help me get through this surgery once again. At least this time I get to stay partially awake so they can watch my heart rate.

See you on the other side.

Elise xx

16th December 2014

Dear Universe,

It was so hard to hold it together at the Year Seven Graduation this evening. Presenting awards to students I have taught for two years straight, and formed such a close bond with, has made it an emotional evening. It was difficult to hold back the tears, saying "Goodbye and good luck" was so hard, especially with what I am dealing with in my own life right now. I knew I couldn't let a tear slip away - if I did, the waterfall wouldn't stop.

My world is falling apart. Why am I so unlovable? My husband of thirteen years has just told me that he doesn't love me anymore and he's leaving me for good this time. He has been threatening for years that he will leave me if I don't do what he or his family wants, but he usually comes back. This time I know he's not. I can't allow myself to be treated like this anymore, even if I am pregnant with his child. His nasty sister hates me and has been telling him to leave me for years. I have never done anything to her or his family, and I don't understand why she dislikes me so much. I think it is because I am too honest and open for her narcissistic games. I have never been accepted by his family; never been good enough for their only son. Even when we were just married, his father would joke that he would find "*a nice Croatian girl for his Croatian son.*" I thought they would like and accept me one day, but it never happened. When I had my heart surgery, I never even got a card or a visit or a skerrick of compassion. They probably hoped I would die, just like their son did. How have I allowed myself to be treated like that for so many years? How have I allowed people to be so nasty? Enough is enough. I won't allow myself to be downtrodden any longer.

Part of me wanted to hear Ivan say those words *"I'm leaving"* as I have suspected it for so long by the way he treats me. But the other part of me feared the confirmation of rejection. The way he looks at me with disgust and vile. The way he has discounted my feelings for so long. The lies and deceit. The sneaky, underhanded actions to purposely do things against me, and the denial of any wrongdoing. The total lack of empathy and compassion and the ongoing, unforgiving emotional neglect. The constant sulking and ignoring me, withholding affection of any kind. The fact is, I am too scared to fall asleep at night in fear that I won't ever wake up again. I wait until he goes to the gym in the early hours of the morning before it feels safe to fall asleep. I live in terror that he will smother my face with a pillow during the night. The way I have been made to feel, that it's all in my head and everything is my fault. It is my fault for not making him love me enough. It is my fault for being born with a congenital heart defect and always being unwell. It is my fault for being a germ freak, knowing a simple cold could kill me. It is my fault that I am 26 weeks pregnant with his child. It is my fault that we are having another girl and I haven't provided him with a son. It is my fault that his family doesn't like me because I don't do things their way. It is my fault that he is not happy.

But is it my fault that I have feelings, emotions and needs that he refuses to acknowledge? Is it my fault for loving such a horrid person and not being strong enough to walk away all of those years ago? Is it my fault for wasting so many years of my precious life with someone so egotistical? How did I not see it? I was never enough for that man and never will be. Not for someone who is incapable of loving anyone other than himself.

I have come to realise that there are people in life that are givers and there are those that are just takers. I know I am a giver. I get joy from giving to and helping others, it's why I chose to be a teacher. I know after giving and giving to someone that is only capable of taking, that I no longer have anything left to give. He's taken it all. Every little ounce of me, he's eaten it away like a cancer. I know I am a skeleton of my once bright and bubbly self who had the world at my feet. What happened? Where did that person go? Will she ever return?

Maybe, as I now face the difficulty of bringing a baby into this world on my own, I will be set free from the years of control, emotional torture and torment. Years and years of emotional neglect and feeling so alone in this world. My body is full of scars on the outside from all my surgeries. People can see those scars and acknowledge the pain. But people have no idea about the scars and pain I carry on the inside, beneath this smile. That is the problem with emotional abuse, you can't see it, especially when it happens behind closed doors, and a facade is put on for the world. All these years, I have been made to believe it's in my head and everything is always my fault. What kind of a man leaves their wife pregnant and takes no responsibility for his actions? Not a man that deserves my love. Please Universe, give me the strength to get through this. I know I need to just put one foot in front of the other and tackle one day at a time. I know I need to keep swimming, just keep swimming for that shoreline. But at the moment, I can't even see the horizon, I am treading water in the deep, dark ocean alone and don't even know which way land lies, or which direction to swim.

Elise xx

5
Solo

3rd February 2015

Dear Universe,

It's 2am and I can't sleep, so I'm writing to you. I can't believe I am going to be bringing a baby into this world solo. I am petrified. I am terrified of the waves that lie ahead. I rest here, 32 weeks pregnant with pains in my stomach. I am so anxious; I can't tell whether they are contractions or just the pit of my stomach turning over in anticipation of the swell that is approaching on the horizon. I am not ready to bring a premature baby into this world on my own. I am putting on a brave face for my daughter's sake, but I don't know how I am going to do this while fighting for custody of the children. I don't know if I have the energy to constantly fight this man, as I know he will never give up until he wins, until he has power and control. He told me he will destroy me. He told me he will do anything to bring me down. What kind of a man leaves their wife pregnant, constantly threatens and tortures the mother of his children emotionally, lies about her to his family and friends and then wants custody of his children? I know how relentless this man is. I know he will do everything in his power to make sure I don't find peace and happiness in my life. I know I can't let that happen, but I know how much energy it is going to take to fight this man forever and to protect my girls from his narcissistic and neglectful emotional abuse. I need to get some rest, because I know tomorrow is going to be a massive day. This baby will be coming into the world, and I refuse to let that man spoil the moment.

Elise xx

4th February 2015

Dear Universe,

I did it! I delivered a premature baby girl into this world today, on my own, solo. I found strength from parts of me that I did not even know I had. I was strong today and I am so proud of getting through it as I did. She is absolutely beautiful and precious. Bringing a baby into the world should be the most joyous and precious time, and I have tried my best to make it that, but I can't deny how traumatic and difficult this has been. She might be a tiny bundle, full of medical tubes right now, but she is strong and spirited, and I can already tell that she is going to be a force to be reckoned with in this world. She was determined to arrive early, feet first!

It started in the early hours of the morning when the pains were getting worse. I waited until I dropped my daughter to school before driving myself to the hospital. I picked Mum up on the way; she can't drive but I needed her moral support. I knew I was having this baby today, whether I wanted to or not. I can't believe I drove myself to hospital in labour! I can hardly remember getting here, just swiftly parking the car directly out the front of the hospital and waddling through the front doors as fast as I could. As soon as the midwife helped me to a bed, she performed the usual lower region inspection and pressed the emergency button for the doctors to come quickly. I looked over at my mother who had burst into tears. She was supposed to be my emotional support, yet here I was being the calm one!

"I just can't understand how a man could do this to my beautiful daughter, look at you, you are bringing a baby into this world prematurely on your own, you have all of these health issues and have already been through so much. I just can't understand how any person could do this to you," she said through tears. I replied calmly, "It's okay, Mum, I am okay, I've got this, I don't want that man or anyone to ruin this special moment for me or my daughter. I want to enjoy this baby coming into the world and I am not going to let anyone take that away."

Before I knew it, I was being wheeled into a disinfected room ready to deliver the baby through an emergency caesarean. The doctor had the large needle ready for my spine. My elderly mother was running alongside the bed trying not to trip over the blue suit she had to quickly drape over her clothes. Everything seemed to be in fast-forward, and I wish I was able to take a breath and take everything in, but it all happened so quickly.

Within moments, I had doctors in the room pulling a tiny baby from my body while Mum was holding my hand. I heard a cry, which was a good sign. That meant she was okay, didn't it? Then I heard silence, complete silence. Medical professionals came rushing into the room and whipped her off into another room within seconds. She had stopped breathing. She was just thirty-two weeks and five days old. She wasn't ready to come into this world yet, even though she thought she was. My mother rushed to be with her. The room emptied out and was suddenly too quiet, it was just me and the doctor and nurse left. They were sewing me up. I lay there in silence, not knowing if my baby was going to be okay.

"Is she going to be okay? She stopped breathing, didn't she?" I asked, tears rolling down my cheeks.

The doctor replied with empathy in her voice, "She is in good hands, and she will be okay. She has been shifted to the NICU unit so she can receive the highest care, but she is now stable. The positive is, everything looks good here, so you should be able to be with her shortly."

Not being able to hold my newborn baby straight after such a traumatic birth was extremely difficult. I was just yearning to hold her and be with her.

As I lay there looking up at the bright lights on the ceiling and the vertical white sheets screening my view of what they were doing to my insides, the enormity of everything struck me like a baseball bat. The tears continued to roll down my cheeks and my body began to shake. As I looked around the sterile white room, hearing the beeping of machines, the memories and triggers from my heart surgery rushed back to me. I wanted to get out of there, but I couldn't even feel my legs. I couldn't move from the waist down. The voices in my head kept telling me to stay calm, that it would all be over shortly. Watching me tremble like a leaf, a nurse came over and covered me with an extra blanket.

"It's likely the medications they've given you, and the emergency birth, that's causing you to shake like this," the nurse claimed, not knowing my story or previous trauma. I lay there in silence and waited patiently for the room to stop moving and for everything to be over. I closed my eyes and imagined I was floating in the calm sea waters on a tropical island. I tried to imagine I was in my happy place, the water. It worked, because before I knew it, I was holding my beautiful daughter in my arms. She was covered in tiny tubes and had bandages on her face and arms. She was beautiful, so innocent and angelic. I kissed her forehead, held her to my chest and whispered in her ear, "Mummy loves you."

I know raising a baby on my own is going to be the hardest thing I will ever do, but I know I can do this. I can raise my girls on my own; I don't need a man, nor do I want one. I just don't know if I have the energy to constantly fight against their father. I know he will never, ever give in until he gets what he wants - power and control.

Elise xx

18th February 2015

Dear Universe,

Today was full of mixed emotions. I was elated to
bring my little baby girl home from hospital after over
two weeks, but I was also terrified at the thought of
doing this all on my own. I have missed my eldest
daughter like crazy and can't wait to spend time with
her again. It used to be just she and I against the world,
as her father was hardly ever home. Her world has
been turned upside down; her parents are divorced and
she has a new baby sister. I am lucky to have my
parents living so close by to help us. They have been
absolutely amazing - I don't know what I would have
done without their help, especially today.

I had only been home for a few hours when it
happened. I was hobbling around the house with the
help of my mum. It was painful to walk. I have had a
caesarean before and remember the pain, but I couldn't
remember it being this sore. I shuffled to the toilet
holding my stomach, in excruciating pain, when my
insides decided to explode all over the bathroom floor.
The stitches in my stomach had burst with pressure
from an internal infection, spilling pus and blood all

over the bathroom and moving internal organs to places they didn't belong. I screamed for my mother's help. I don't know who was in more shock, Mum or me. She called Dad immediately and before I knew it, we were back in hospital.

As I lay there once again on a hospital bed, hooked up to a drip with surgeons looking at my insides, I glanced over at my elderly father, sitting by my side cradling my precious baby girl in his arms . How grateful I am to call that wonderful man my dad. Always calm and full of wisdom; my rock, my protector. The one man in my life that has always been there for me.

As I looked at him peacefully rocking my baby girl, I contemplated that if I would ever find such a man to be by my side, having someone even a fraction of the person that he is, it would be a blessing. I pondered my chances and have come to the realisation that I am alone in this world and the sooner I come to terms with that, the better. No man is ever going to want me with all of my baggage - an excess suitcase of medical conditions, ghastly scars and two kids to raise!

Elise xx

6
Memory Lane

21st October 2017

Dear Universe,

I could feel the nerves in my stomach as I walked into the party alone. I haven't really socialised since my divorce, as I've been raising a baby on my own. Who has a divorce party anyway? I have never been to one before and wasn't sure what to expect. I knew there wouldn't be too many familiar faces there as it had been many years since graduating high school.

As I accepted a drink and started chatting to people, I was surprised to see some ladies I hadn't seen since 1996 – twenty-one years ago. What is it with the number 21! As we began talking and sharing life stories, it became difficult to share mine. Being left pregnant after heart failure and open-heart surgery doesn't exactly slip into conversation easily. These ladies weren't from high school, they were friends from Sailing Camp. A time in my life when things seemed easy. A time when I dreamed of the life ahead of me. Where did it all go wrong? Those times seemed like yesterday. Where had all those years gone? Wasted, misused time I will never get back.

The ladies started walking over towards me smiling, "Elise! I haven't seen you in years, you still look the same. You haven't changed a bit."
"Hello Anna and Felicia, you both look wonderful, what a blast from the past!" I answered.
As we sat down and start chatting about the superficial things in life, like where we live, what we do for work, how many children we have, I couldn't help but feel this weird feeling of Deja vu. It was difficult to think of the past and what may have been, and to see the wonderful things other people have done and not compare them to my own life. It was challenging to walk down memory lane when I know that I wasted so many years of my life with someone that despised me. Someone that was jealous and envious of me in every way possible and would do everything in his power to make sure I didn't succeed in life and show him up. I was pondering what my life would have been like if I had made different choices. These ladies seemed happy with their lives. It got me wondering if it was all a facade, or whether people can actually be genuinely happy with their life choices. When did life get so

complicated? Raising a family on my own wasn't part of the plan. I never wanted this; I never wanted my kids to go through this. How can these ladies seem so happy and be celebrating their life at a divorce party, of all things?

It wasn't long before I looked at my watch and realised I had to leave the party already. I had a toddler and child to get home to. The guilt of motherhood and the sacrifices made, aways putting our children's needs before our own, is something only a mother would understand. Being a single mum, doing this all on my own, isn't easy. Having no one to share the load with is exhausting and having an ex that works against me rather than with me makes things even more difficult. As I said my goodbyes to these acquaintances from the past, they asked if I was on social media so they could stay in contact.

I smiled and replied with, "Of course, I finally succumbed to the world of Facebook!" Little did they know that my ex-husband wouldn't allow me to join, and it was only now that I have been able to make contact with people from the past.

By the time I got home I had three friend requests waiting for approval. After I got into bed I scrolled through the social media accounts of these lovely

women and their warm messages about our evening
reminiscing. I couldn't help but wonder how or why I
lost contact with them along the way, and it got me
thinking about Sailing Camp again. I went through
their friends lists to see if I could remember any of
them and there it was ... Steven Thompson. My heart
skipped a beat. I hadn't thought of him in a very long
time. A strange feeling came over me. I wanted to
click on his profile, but I also didn't want to open that
door to what might have been if the universe had been
listening all those years ago. But I couldn't resist the
temptation to click and stalk. There were photos of him
and his children living a perfect life. He's obviously
married - I heard many years ago that he married
someone from Sailing Camp.

It was a weird sense of new beginnings and
reminiscing tonight. Was meeting people I hadn't seen
in over twenty years a sign? Is it supposed to mean
something? I don't know. Sometimes it is coincidence,
but sometimes I feel this sense that you are trying to
tell me something, Universe. So tonight, I did
something I would normally never do. I didn't
overthink it, I didn't overanalyse like I usually do. I
just did it. Click! I sent Steven a friend request. He
probably won't answer, but that's okay. Tonight, I just

followed my gut and the signs from the universe, something I need to do more often.

Elise xx

29th October 2017

Dear Universe,

You won't believe what happened today. I was at the park with my girls and heard the beep of my phone. As I glanced down and read the notification across the screen, my heart skipped a beat. *Steven Thompson has accepted your friend request. Steven Thompson has sent you a message.* I couldn't believe it! I had totally forgotten about even sending that request last week. My heart started beating faster as I read the messages from him. Could this be a sign from the universe?

Within minutes, we were messaging back and forth and being jovial, just like things were twenty-one years ago. He's divorced! He is recently divorced! I can't believe it. I mean, I am happy to just make a friend with someone going through the same thing as me, no expectations. But I must admit, it feels like I am living in a time warp. It feels so strange going back to the past, but it's also my comfort zone. He asked if I want to catch up for a drink. I presume he just means as friends, it's not a date or anything. Just friends catching up. There is nothing wrong with that is there?
Elise xx

1st November 2017

Dear Universe,

It is a really strange feeling. Today I met Steven,
someone I met twenty-one years ago and felt a
connection with. I know it was only a teenage crush,
but I have often thought about him over the years and
wondered how life has treated him. After all this time,
I couldn't believe I was meeting him once again. I felt
the butterflies in my stomach as I waited nervously at
the Beachside Café for him to arrive. This wasn't even
a date, it was just two acquaintances catching up,
comparing stories of divorce.

I could see a man with a ponytail walking towards the
café, and even though the distance made it hard to see
the details in his face, I could tell it was him by his
walk. As he got closer, I could make out the features of
his face and I knew it was him. He seemed very
different to how I remembered him - or maybe it was
that he wasn't sixteen anymore! I didn't really know
what to expect, but the Steven I remember was an
athletic, talented, cheeky and happy surfie. This Steven
seemed very different; he was a fully grown man with
facial hair and children! He was no longer a teenager,

unsure of his place in the world. I could sense by his face the years of sadness that life had dealt him. Detecting his nerves as he politely hugged me, I cheerfully greeted him with a smile and did my best to help him relax. I tend to do that; I always try and make things easier for people when I know they are nervous or struggling socially. I think it's the years of welcoming nervous students into my classroom and doing my best to make them feel at home, but I also think it's my empathy and compassion, putting the needs of others first and often neglecting my own.

We chatted and talked about life, children and divorce. I had this weird gut feeling that something was amiss with him. He wasn't the person I once knew - or was it my expectations, or the way I remembered him? My gut was telling me something today and I couldn't quite work out what it was - or maybe I didn't want to. It felt like he was hiding something, or isn't being truthful, but I can't work out if that is the mistrust from my own trauma and triggers of the past. He seemed jittery and on edge, and I noticed his hands were shaking at times. A tracheostomy scar was clear on his neck, but I didn't want to ask what it was from. I know he never had it at sixteen, and I had a funny feeling that there was much more to this story. I felt a negative vibe and aura coming from him, it scared me a little but I didn't know why. Maybe it's that he admitted that he suffers from depression and if I am honest, mental health disorders scare me a little. I should be feeling on top of the world, but I'm not. I can feel the energy draining from me. Maybe I'm simply scared, or maybe my gut is trying to tell me something. I don't know, I can't tell the difference.

We reminisced about the days of Sailing Camp and how quickly time had passed. We ended the evening with a beach walk. Steven carried my shoes in one hand and grabbed hold of my hand with the other. The sound of the waves crashing to the shore and the reflections of moonlight on the water made for a romantic setting. Suddenly, Steven leaned in and kissed me. At first, I didn't know what to think. I was in shock. How could this happen after all this time? What a time warp I was in. I didn't know what to think or feel. I felt numb. I should have been feeling happy and excited, but I wasn't. I was scared.

I can't work out if I am scared to let down my walls that protect me from getting hurt, or if I am sensing something that isn't right. Is the universe trying to tell me something? I am questioning everything, overthinking everything. I am confused. I am feeling the need to swim away from the shore. I don't feel this is right for me, but I feel comfort in the past and the known, rather than the unknown waters. I want companionship and I guess the universe wouldn't put him in my path once again unless he was meant to be there, but it was me that made that contact, not him. Does that mean I should have closed that door and let it be? Is the universe telling me to run? This is all too hard; I don't know what to do. Maybe delving back into the past wasn't such a good idea.

Elise xx

9th November 2017

Dear Universe,

The weather was overcast, but the heat coming off the sand kept me warm while I was waiting. He was late - not a good start to our second date. I can't stand lateness and it's a pet hate of mine as my ex-husband was always late. I think it's a sign of selfishness. When he finally arrived in a singlet and thongs, I couldn't help but feel he had made very little effort to prepare for the date. To fly the red flag even further, it turned out he was late because he was selling some of his belongings, which means he's tight on money. I know that money doesn't buy happiness, but I can't help but feel this is another sign that something is not right.

It has only been a week but things have happened so quickly. We have called and chatted each day and he wants to see me again. I think he's falling in love with me already, I can feel it. It scares me a bit, because I can sense he needs me, and I am scared to need or want him. It is nice to feel needed and wanted, something I haven't felt in a very long time. I can't help but feel wary though; those gut feelings just won't go away. I keep telling them to stop and go away, but I don't trust him, and trust is a big thing for me. Maybe I will never trust anyone ever again. I know these gut feelings are only trying to protect me, and it is due to my past hurt and trauma that I am feeling so cautious and suspicious. How do I know if these signs from the universe are telling me something? How do I know what is real and what isn't? I mean, I don't really want to get married again or live with someone or settle down; I don't want to get myself into the situation I was in during my marriage. I couldn't deal with the hurt, emotional trauma, and rejection all over again. My girls come first, and they always will. So this low commitment type of relationship, where we only catch up occasionally, will suit me. He lives his life and I live mine. Perhaps this is what I need and deserve.

Navigating life after divorce with kids is difficult enough, let alone another relationship. I am a romantic at heart, but I am also a realist. I am so confused right now, I don't know if the universe is giving me signs or if it is just me being scared. I don't know what to do.

Elise xx

7

Trust your Gut

15th June 2018

Dear Universe,

The light from the lounge was peering into the bedroom through the half-closed door. It was 2am. Why was he still awake? Why hadn't he gone to bed yet? I walked quietly down the hallway into the spare room where he had set up for the night. As I entered the room unannounced, I startled him. He quickly jumped up and shoved an item into his bag. I knew he was hiding something.

"You're still up? You can't sleep?" I asked.

"Just prepping for the gig tomorrow," Steven's eyes were glazed and his pupils dilated. I knew he had taken something. He always said he was so anti-drugs and I know he didn't drink alcohol as it triggered his depression further, but why was my gut telling me that something was amiss? Am I being paranoid? Is my mistrust a trigger from my past or is my body trying to tell me something?

This morning when I walked into the garage I found a tiny, clear empty bag on the concrete floor near the

64

wheel of his car. I knew as soon as I picked it up that it had held drugs or medications of some kind. I confronted him straight away.

"Can you explain why I just found this in my garage?" He was shocked by my discovery, and I knew he was lying with his response. He wouldn't make eye contact with me and was quick to deflect the situation. I could see the beads of sweat forming on his forehead.

"Geez, it looks like a drug packet, where did you find that?" he replied. "I did give a lift to some young guys from volleyball the other night, so maybe it was theirs and it's fallen out of my car."

I felt sick to my stomach. I didn't believe what he was telling me, and I couldn't understand why he was lying. I could not fathom how or why he would be taking drugs when he was so anti-drugs and didn't even drink alcohol. It didn't make sense. How could this be happening?

I didn't want to drive him to the gig today, but it was too late to cancel. If he was lying to me, what was I to do? I couldn't prove my thoughts and gut feelings.

Watching him play guitar up on stage today, I could tell he was jittery and buzzing. I know he didn't sleep last night, so I couldn't imagine how he was even standing there on stage. On both the drive there and home, there was lots of silence. He knew there was something wrong because I seemed distant. He knew I didn't believe him. All I could think about was everything that I have been through. If he really cared for me as much as he said he did, how could he lie to me and hide something? I felt nervous to the core, but I also felt calm in knowing that the truth will come out eventually. The truth will always prevail.

Elise xx

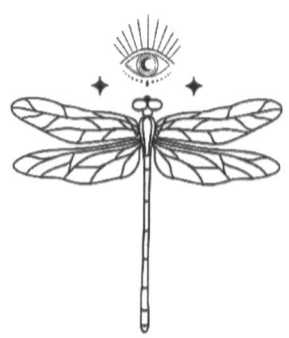

17th June 2018

Dear Universe,

Bang, Bang, Bang! The aggressive knocking on the door could be felt throughout the house. I knew it was him. He didn't have an aggressive bone in his body, but I also knew that for him, times had become desperate. There was no more hiding the truth; this whole situation would have been eating him up on the inside. I hadn't answered his texts or calls; I'd told him I needed space.

I peered through the curtains and noticed his car parked on the verge. I was reluctant to open the door. I didn't want to speak to him, given the recent circumstances, but he was persistent.
"I can't be alone right now. I am feeling really low and scared to be by myself," he pleaded.

I slowly opened the door to a very tired man. Steven looked like something the cat had dragged in; he was unshaven, hair messed up to one side like he had just woken up, and there were stains on his shirt.

He seemed scared and agitated, which concerned me. I hadn't mentioned anything more about the weekend and what I found. I didn't accuse him of lying. I let him come in and sit down. I could tell he was a broken man. I could tell his world had fallen apart. I could tell the truth was about to present itself.

He sat with his face in his hands, his shoulders moving with the tears.

"I need to tell you something and I need you to listen. I have lied to you, and I am so sorry. I can't even get the words out of my mouth because I am so ashamed. But those gut feelings you had about me early on, they were right.. I know you know the truth about the package you found … so why don't you ask me?" he begged.

"Ask you what Steven? I'm not going to make this easy for you - if you have something to say, then it's your truth to tell." I kept my voice calm.

He couldn't stop crying. Even though the situation was all his own doing, I couldn't help but feel for the broken man sitting before me.

"I don't deserve your kindness. I use medications to numb the feeling of depression but it's got out of hand.

I'm taking anything I can get my hands on to help me feel better. I am so ashamed. I need help."

I felt sick. My gut feelings were right. I should have trusted them. I had to hold it together, stay calm and be strong, even though tears were rolling down my cheeks. I was so grateful the kids weren't home.

"Well, thank you for finally being honest. That would have been difficult to admit. I know you won't want this, but I am going to call your sister. You need to go and stay with her so she can help you. I can't help you, and I can't do this anymore." Steven continued to sob while I made the difficult phone call to his sister. She was in shock, and couldn't have been more surprised than I had been. However, I don't understand why I was so shocked when I had this gut feeling all along. I think it is the difference between thoughts and reality. Her support and understanding was a relief and I sent him on his way to her place, hoping he would arrive safely.

It is heart-wrenching to see someone so desperate and broken, even if it is the consequence of their own actions and choices.

As soon as I closed that door, I knew I could never open it to him again. This goodbye was going to be a lasting one. The hardest part is going to be finding the strength to not be pulled back into the whirlpool once again. My strength of wanting to help people can also be my weakness.

I feel angry, hurt and sad all at once. Angry and hurt that I got myself in this situation through being naive and trusting, and sad at what depression has taken away from such a talented and great person. Steven clearly felt he had no way out other than to rely on (unprescribed or illegal) drugs to ease his pain; his addiction got out of hand, and he has now hit rock-bottom. It is precious time wasted, and I only wish he'd had the right help to face his demons from the start. I need to try and somehow understand. If that man only knew how talented he is, and what amazing things he could achieve with the right help and support.

It can be frustrating and exhausting supporting someone with severe depression when you can clearly see their worth and potential. It takes every ounce of your being to be supportive and compassionate. Steven tells me that I couldn't imagine how difficult it is for someone suffering with depression, as they know the impact they are having on everyone around them. This just makes them dive into darkness even deeper. For many, depression is a horrible dark fog that just won't clear. I wish there was a cure. I wish there was more help and hope out there for everyone suffering depression. I wish the world was a more compassionate, kind and caring place for those suffering. I wish I could take all of Steven's pain and darkness away, but I can't.

I am confused. My kindness, compassion and understanding nature makes it difficult to be assertive and to see situations clearly, yet my drive and ambition and will to succeed in life makes it tricky for me to be patient and tolerant. I know what I need to do, but I don't feel like I have the courage. I also know I fear change, so being courageous is going to create change that I might struggle to cope with.

I keep doubting myself and the way forward. I overthink everything. I ask the universe for guidance, but just when there is a sign, I overanalyse what it might mean and I'm back to square one. I need time to process everything, to recentre my thoughts and decide what I need to do. Life is about choices. We do our best to make the right ones, but sometimes we get it wrong. Sometimes we know what the right choice is, but it is too difficult to face, so we avoid it for as long as we can - until we can't evade it any longer.

Elise xx

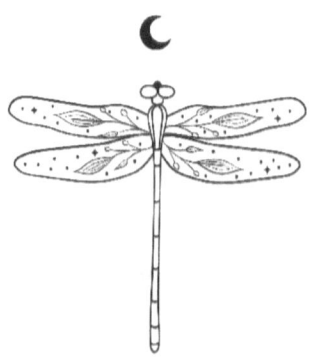

8

Tarot

18th June 2018

Dear Universe,

I visited a Tarot reader this evening, something I didn't think I would ever do. I don't think I've ever really believed in psychics and Tarot reading, but I've definitely developed a fascination about the spiritual world. I often sense a presence from the spirit world. I know it sounds crazy, but I sometimes feel like my grandmother is looking out for me. I can sense her presence. It's weird, I wasn't that close to my grandparents as I was still young when they passed. They didn't really know me, so I find it strange that they might be watching over me.

I did have an out-of-body experience or connection with the spiritual world when I had my heart surgery. I don't talk about it as people would think I am crazy. I watched my whole surgery from above my body. It was like I was floating on the ceiling looking down, watching the surgeons take my heart out of my body, which was covered in silver foil. I could see my blood pumping through tubes and machines from the heart bypass machine. I remember the surgeon receiving a phone call at 4.44pm from my physician wanting an update on the progress of the operation. On my follow-up appointment with the surgeon months later, I asked him if he received a phone call from my doctor while he was operating. He confirmed that he did receive a phone call from my doctor, after he had been operating for over five hours. He couldn't understand how I would know that. During my recovery I researched what the numbers 444 meant. It is a powerful and significant message from your angels and the universe, often seen as a sign of good luck and positive change, a reminder that your angels and the universe are with you, supporting you and guiding you on your path.

From that moment, something awakened in me and I have been taking notice of numbers and signs from the universe ever since. I am no longer oblivious to the signs from the world around me, I look for them and try and understand them.

The Tarot reader is a woman called Sue, who used to work at the same school I did. Her new business kept coming up in my Facebook feed, so I took it as a sign.

Although I never really got to know her that well, I could tell she was a kind, caring and compassionate soul. It didn't surprise me that she feels a connection with the spirit world.

I was a little nervous before I arrived, as I wasn't sure what to expect. The overthinking started to take over. *What if she tells me things I don't want to hear? What am I even doing here?* As soon as I arrived and saw Sue's kind eyes, I felt myself relax. I hadn't told her much about myself, but I could tell she already knew the type of person I was, and that life had thrown challenges my way. I felt connected to her, like she understood me. I think we share some similarities in our journeys.

Sue got me to shuffle and divide the pack of cards before she dealt them out onto the table. Then she slowly turned them over, looking closely at each card and spending time with each one. She asked me questions as she explained what she thought the cards meant. I couldn't help but feel there was lots of darkness in those cards and her reading, but I knew she was trying to create positivity from it. I could sense a glum feeling from the cards before me and that it was likely representing the situation I was currently in.

"Did you know your grandmother is sitting beside you? She has dark eyes and dark hair." I was stunned. How could that be true? How could she tell? I hadn't told her about the feeling I've had that my grandmother is watching over me.

I couldn't hold back the tears that started rolling down my cheek. Why was she watching over me? She didn't know me that well, but I have always felt a connection to her side of the family and my Dutch heritage.

"You are very spiritual and in tune. You are a sensitive soul. I can feel it."

I have always felt that. I know I am very intuitive and I feel things deeply. So what she said is true.

The reading wasn't able to tell me much that I didn't already know, but I think there have been things I don't want to face or believe. I don't feel I really got any answers of what I need to do, and I am still confused about everything. Sue kept telling me that I was on the right path and that I need to keep moving forward. All the signs suggest I *am* on the right path. But where is this path going? There were things that resonated with me though. She said when I am ready, I need to let the universe clearly know, and it will give me signs. But I write to you all the time, Universe, how do I get you to hear me? How am I going to know when I am ready? How do I make myself ready for whatever you have in store for me?

On the drive home, I of course overanalysed everything that she said and what the cards might mean. I thought about what has happened in my life and why I was in this situation. Why was I so terrible at choosing men? Why did I let myself be lied to and deceived? Why am I so naive and trusting? Why isn't everyone straight forward and honest like me? I need to look at myself and the choices I keep making. I am a kind and caring soul, but is there a way of developing assertiveness that won't jeopardise that?

I did a lot of thinking this evening after the Tarot reading, and I feel I *am* on the right path. Maybe I have just had to learn these lessons the hard way. Maybe I have had to learn that sometimes love isn't always enough. Maybe the connections we make with people happen to teach us a lesson. And maybe tonight's Tarot lesson has given me more than I first thought!

I have come to a few realisations. We can't walk forward while looking backwards, as that would mean we are moving backwards. We can't look ahead if we are focusing on the past. That doesn't mean reflection on the past isn't a good thing - it is. Reflection brings perspective and growth, but we need to be careful not to be consumed by the past, as that is wasted energy. Sometimes it is easier for us to go back into our comfort zone. It is easier to go back to people we once knew, as it is familiar to us, it feels safer, but it isn't always the safe or wise thing to do. We often fear change, fear the unknown. To grow as individuals, we need to face our fears of change and imperfection, and to make mistakes along the way in order to know which direction to grow.

I felt clarity from my reading this evening. I feel I am on the right path, even if there is a difficult and lonely journey ahead. I know what I need to do. The water isn't as murky, the surging currents are a little calmer, and I just need to keep swimming ahead for that tropical island and not look back. Even if the past wants to drag me back with the tide, I need to keep swimming forward.

Elise xx

9

Forgive & Let Go

21 June 2019

Dear Universe,

I've been receiving constant phone calls and texts from Steven, begging for forgiveness. He says he was in a deep, dark depression and wasn't thinking right, and that he would do anything to make things work. I don't doubt that he cares about me, and I don't doubt that he regrets his choices. I also don't doubt that he wants to right his wrongs and live a life of truth and purpose, but I do doubt that we were right for each other. I know if I had listened to my gut feelings to begin with, none of this would have even happened. The universe kept telling me, but I didn't want to listen. I know our reconnection had a purpose. I believe it was my responsibility to help him. His parting words to me were, "You are my angel, you saved my life and for that I will be forever grateful."
Maybe that is true, and I did help guide him back onto the right path.

I know it seems naive considering the lies and deceit, but I wholeheartedly forgive him for the pain and hurt he's caused me. I know he didn't do it intentionally. He had his own demons to fight before our paths even crossed again, and they had nothing to do with me. I know I have helped him find his way in this world, just as he has helped me find mine. He is a kind soul with so much to offer this world. I hope one day he is able to see himself through different eyes. I hope one day he finds happiness.

This afternoon, I went to my happy place. I drove down to the beach and sat on the soft white sand watching the waves slowly kiss the shore. Being the middle of winter it was too cold to swim, but there was no breeze and the sun was trying its best to peer through the clouds. I watched the water slowly sieve through the sand in tiny bubbles. I looked out to the horizon, I breathed in the fresh sea air and found solace. And there it was, lying on the sand next to me,- another sign from the universe. A dead dragonfly on the sand, its blue wings moving lightly in the breeze. It felt like a reminder that you can't keep living in the past - you need to move on and let go.

The universe puts people on our path to teach us lessons about ourselves. Maybe Steven and I reconnecting again had the purpose of teaching each other an important lesson in life. I can't make him change for the better, nor is it my responsibility to. He must want to create positive changes to better himself. He needs to travel this journey alone, as I need to travel this part of my journey solo. I have so much to learn about myself and I know it's going to be okay. No matter how hard we try, we can't force things that aren't meant for us. It is why you can't force things that aren't working. Loving someone is not controlling them, it's letting go. True unconditional love is appreciating someone for who they are and not trying to change them, it's loving them and accepting them wholeheartedly for what makes them who they are. But loving and caring for someone doesn't mean that you are meant to be together or even in each other's lives. Sometimes, we need to love someone from afar. Sometimes, we need to let go and say goodbye, even if it seems impossible to do.

People say relationships aren't always easy and they all can require effort. This is true, but doesn't everything in life require effort to be successful? What you put in, you get back. If you follow your passions and do the things you love, it doesn't feel like work. Relationships are no different, if you are with the right person, it doesn't seem like work or effort. Listen to the universe and the signs that it presents.

The universe is telling me I need to say goodbye. The universe is telling me that I need to forgive, let go and move forward. The universe is telling me that I need to swim this channel solo and have faith that the waters will guide me to the right destination. This time, I am choosing to listen to the universe.

Elise xx

10
Swipe Right

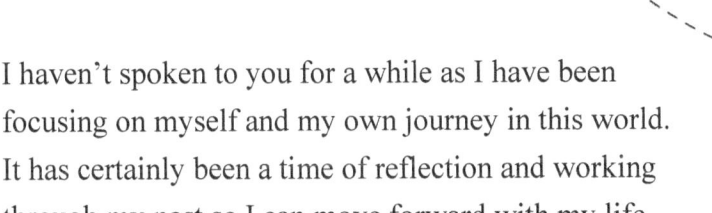

21st May 2021

Dear Universe,

I haven't spoken to you for a while as I have been focusing on myself and my own journey in this world. It has certainly been a time of reflection and working through my past so I can move forward with my life.

Last night, sitting on the shower floor, my relentless tears melded with the warm shower water. I just couldn't stop crying. I was alone. The kids are at their dad's house this weekend and the loneliness had hit me. In some ways I have welcomed the solitude; I have wanted and needed to be alone. But last night in the shower, it was like all the years of pain and torment made their way out. I have had no choice but to keep swimming against the current for all these years; I never had time to stop. I couldn't, I knew if I did, I would sink. I had to keep my head above the surface and keep swimming, as I knew if I was to stop moving, I was going to sink to the bottom. But this weekend, I feel like the universe has forced me to stop. To process everything that has happened. To grieve. To let myself feel and to be at peace with the past, so I can finally let myself heal and move forward with my life. As the tears finally started to dwindle, I thought about the words Sue had said to me in my Tarot reading, about letting the universe know when I am ready. I looked up to the heavens from the bathroom floor and yelled, "I am ready Universe, please, I am ready!"

This morning I woke up with the strange feeling that my life is about to change. Part of me is scared, part of me is excited, part of me is having to trust in you, Universe. I am finally at peace with everything, and I know my direction going forward. I know what I deserve and what I want from this world and the kind of footprint that I want to leave behind.

I made myself a morning coffee and headed outside to brave the cold early-morning sun. There was a little friend waiting for me on the back door. This time it wasn't a dead one, it was very much alive. The bluest and prettiest dragonfly I have ever seen, waiting patiently to fly. The sun was glistening on its wings, creating an opal-like sheen. I know this beautiful blue dragonfly was a sign from the universe. What it represents, I don't know, but I can feel it is something to do with change and new beginnings.

It must be something about the number 21 – today is the 21st of the month. I am learning to watch, listen and learn the signs of the universe. Dragonflies upon my path, guiding the way. I can sense the shift in my world. I can feel the change, but I can't quite describe it completely. I can feel the negativity lifting from my shoulders. I think it is because I have finally accepted that I don't really like change. Change brings uncertainty, and with that brings fear, but it also brings opportunity and growth. I am pushing myself to step out of my comfort zone. I know that life is to be lived and I need to trust that the universe will bring me what I deserve when I am living the best life I possibly can, full of purpose and truth. I am ready; I am ready to love and be loved.

Elise xx

16th May 2021

Dear Universe,

"Swipe right. Just swipe right!" I could hear the universe whispering in my ear. What the hell am I doing on a dating app at the age of forty? I am too old for this crap. As I was continually swiping left on the unimpressive profiles before me, there was one profile I couldn't help but pause on. Someone that stood out to me from the crowd that was different to what I would usually look for in a man. Although it is not as though what I have looked for before has worked for me, has it!

He's handsome, very cute, with a sense of calmness and a down-to-earth nature. How can you tell this from a few photos and a brief biography? I don't know, but I just have this positive gut feeling. I can't put my finger on it, but I am just going to go with it. I am going to trust my gut with this one. I swiped right.

This evening I got a notification on my phone at exactly 21:21pm. *You have a match!* I knew this was another sign. I knew it was him. Sure enough, our profiles matched. *Do I send the first message or does he?* I decided I wasn't going to overthink it like I usually do, so I just sent a quick '*Hello,*' and our chatting began. He seems lovely. Very honest and genuine. He's already asked me on a date next weekend. I can't wait to meet him. Usually, I would be so nervous about this sort of thing but I feel strangely calm. Like I am just trusting in you, Universe. If things are meant to be, they will be.

Elise xx

22nd May 2021

Dear Universe,

I just had the loveliest first date with James. He is so well-mannered and genuine but very down-to-earth. An absolute gentleman. I can tell his parents have raised him well, but I can also tell he's cheeky and has lived life. I find that attractive, the perfect mix of responsible and mischievous. We got along really well and within moments I felt at ease around him, as if I had known him for many years. His honest and open nature helped me feel at home. It also helps that he's an over-sharer like me, it makes me feel I can trust him.

Hopefully, I didn't put him off with my comment that I wasn't interested in getting married again or moving in with someone. I could tell he was a little taken back when I said it, but seemed to laugh it off. Probably not the best thing to say to someone on the first date, but it just came out! I think I can't help but put a wall up and protect myself from getting hurt.

We chatted and laughed over lunch, and feeling so comfortable made time go so quickly. As the date was coming to an end, we walked to the front of the restaurant. He kindly paid for the bill, and when he handed over his credit card, I noticed his large hands. They reminded me of my grandfather's - tanned and weathered from hard outdoor work.

The rain was pelting down outside, and water was overflowing off the veranda. We stood together on the terrace, waiting for the rain to settle. I noticed how cleanly presented he was, and how much his smile overshadowed the dreary weather. His big blue eyes were kind and his face openly showed expression. He was a happy soul with a good sense of humour. I could tell he enjoyed life; there was a confidence in his grin I found intriguing. As we stood together sheltering from the rain, I noticed he was looking up at me.

"Does it bother you that I'm not that tall?" he asked.

I promptly and honestly replied, "No, not at all, does it bother you that I have size 12 feet?"

He laughed. I don't care about his height or his wage or any superficial crap. I am interested in getting to know him as a person and I can only hope he is interested in getting to know me.

As I hugged him goodbye, thanking him for such a lovely day, I got a whiff of his cologne. It was heavenly, he smelled divine. They say smell is a good indicator of attraction. His voice made me feel calm and comforted. He walked me to my car like a gentleman and gave me one last hug in the sprinkling rain as we parted ways. I took one last sniff of his heavenly aroma and beamed. As I started my car and the windscreen wipers began moving to the rhythm of the rain, I sat for a moment to process what had just happened. I smiled. I had such a good feeling about today, only good vibes. Positivity is in the air! I really want to see him again, but it is out of my hands and up to the universe. I just need to be patient and wait and see.

I will send him a text to thank him and let him know I had a lovely time and that I would love to see him again. That is me, honest and upfront. I can already tell he is the same. So, if he wants to see me again, he will - if not, then so be it. You can't force these things.

Elise xx

18th June 2021

Dear Universe,

Last night, we chatted for hours while cuddling on the couch. I knew I was a goner. This man has my heart - hook, line, and sinker. As he held me in his arms and looked into my eyes with pure love, I could sense that he felt the same way I did. As his big blue eyes glistened against the reflection of the mood lighting in his apartment, I could see slight tears welling in his eyes, as much as I could feel them rising in mine. I could sense those wonderous words … *I love you*, but neither of us said a word, we didn't need to.

Knowing that it must be getting late, I glanced down at my phone. It was 1.11 am. Do the numbers 111 mean something? I keep seeing them a lot lately. I have heard it is an angel number or something indicating new beginnings. Maybe it's a sign. James was begging me to stay, and I didn't want to leave, but I wasn't quite ready for overnight yet - not ready for him to see me vulnerable in the morning with no makeup on! I feel like we never have enough time together, it goes too quickly. I count the hours until we see each other again and can't help but wind the window down and ask for just one more kiss before I drive away. Where has this man been all my life? Why couldn't I have met him all those years ago? How different would my life have been?

Elise xx

21st June 2021

Dear Universe,

What a whirlwind of a month it has been! Last night James stayed over for the first time ever. We finally said those special words to each other. I am still on cloud nine. I have never felt anything like it in my life. I cannot even describe the chemistry and connection I have with this man. I did not even know that such a thing even existed. It is like looking in the mirror of your soul and seeing and feeling that refection of you in someone else. That sense that you have known this person before, and they know and understand you without having to talk or explain. A glance, a sigh, or a brush of the hand, and I know what he's feeling. I know he feels it too. He is my soulmate, my twin flame, I have no doubt. Not a doubt in the world. Nothing has been forced, it has just happened naturally. It is the first time in my life that I have felt so sure about anything. Handsome, honest, genuine, reliable, trustworthy, kind, funny, down-to-earth, caring, giving - what more could a girl want?! We share the same morals and values, and our goals and future aspirations line up. I didn't realise how important that is in a partner, sharing the same vision.

You can be two different people but share the same ethics and dreams. James isn't intimidated by my intelligence, nor is he jealous or envious. He is attracted to my desire to constantly learn and he is grateful to have me by his side. That is a nice feeling, not having to hide who I am and be truly appreciated. He looks up to successful people, not wanting to bring them down like the 'tall poppy syndrome' so many people in our society seem to possess these days.

I finally know what it feels like to love and be loved. To be truly and utterly loved and adored for the person I am and to love someone in return with every ounce of my being. Finally, I can see out to the horizon. The fog has lifted. I can see the future and sense the hope, love, and happiness in the sunrise. For the first time in a very long time, I feel free and empowered. It is because I have trusted my gut, taking notice from the signs of the universe. For the first time in a long time, I am not swimming against the current, nor treading water. I am floating in the calm and serene waters, looking out to the clear horizon. This time, I am not alone. I am hand in hand with the love of my life.

Elise xx

29th July 2021

Dear Universe,

This weekend has been one of the most memorable and unforgettable times in my life. Poignant and special in so many ways. It has been my child-free weekend, usually a time of worry and anxiety that my girls will be okay without me, but this weekend was all about yours truly and the ability to be spontaneous and free spirited; something I can't remember feeling since I was a teenager, and in many ways, I don't know if I ever was able to be completely free, as I have always felt the need to be responsible and selfless.

James has been on a trip up north that was planned before we met. I have been missing him like crazy; two weeks without being in his arms has seemed like forever. He surprised me with plane tickets to join him in magical Karijini. I have never been on a plane by myself before, or even travelled alone. As I wheeled my suitcase into the early-morning darkness, eagerly awaiting to board the plane, I felt like a child again. Lost yet excited, nervous yet eager, naive yet free. I can't remember the last time I felt like this, if ever.

As I settled into my window seat, I felt the butterflies in my stomach flutter as the loud engines started to rumble. Travelling solo is scary, but exhilarating. Becoming a mum and always putting the needs of others first has made it difficult for me to rediscover the joys of life. Through no fault of my own, my situations have made it so hard for me to feel free or be completely myself. Where did Elise go for all of those years? Where did that fun-loving and spirited girl disappear to? Financial constraints, ongoing health issues and parental responsibilities have stopped her from living life. I am glad she has finally returned.

A quick flight, just over an hour. We were landing soon after take-off. As I peered through the plane's small window, I could see red dust as far as the eye could see. Walking out on the tarmac in the middle of barren land, I looked at the red hills surrounding the runway. It was a typical Australian landscape of gum trees and red dirt. The soft breeze brought the scent of eucalyptus leaves in the dry heat. It wasn't long now until I was in his arms. I could feel the anticipation and excitement as I collected my luggage and boarded the shuttle bus to town.

The scenery - red cliffs, spinifex grass and large trees - reminded me I was far away from home, but little did I know that I hadn't even started to see the full wonders of this part of the country. As the bus pulled in, I could see James waiting with a smile. My heart skipped a beat, and my eyes welled with tears. I couldn't wait to jump into his arms, breathe in his divine aroma and kiss his soft lips.

There was no time to waste. We set up camp and headed out on the road to see the marvels of Karijini. How I had missed his company and being in his safe embrace. Our conversations were always endless and there were never enough minutes in the day together.

Karijini is truly breathtaking, a trip I will never forget. Lush green forest on the banks of large red cliffs, encircling lagoons and waterfalls. The awe of that place is something you can't describe until you experience it. How lucky are we that nature has created such a masterpiece? As we trekked, we chatted and held hands like we had just met. As we approached the beauty of Fern Pool, my usual worries and anxieties seemed to have disappeared. I couldn't wait to dive into the water, even if it did look cold. The fog from the cool air was misting on the turquoise-blue waters and the reflections of green ferns surrounded the lagoon. The trickling sounds of water filtering through the red cliff echoed across the cove. I was the first to take the plunge; James took a lot more convincing. The water was freezing, but the experience was well worth it. Such a magical feeling, being in the water, my happy place, with the love of my life in the wonders of Karijini. An experience I will never ever forget.

I think the most significant part about this magical weekend with James has not only been the romance and travels, but finding myself again. Rediscovering the joys of life has been liberating. After arriving back home, I contemplated the wonderful trip I had just experienced and felt the need to send a message and some photos to Sue, the Tarot reader, who I now consider a friend. I thought of her and the role she played in helping me to understand my path in this world. I sent her my favourite pic of James and me in Karijini along with a message saying:

Hey Sue,

Just wanted to say a big thank you for all your help and support over the last few years. I asked the universe and it delivered. I have definitely met my soulmate. Absolutely no doubts!

Elise xx

This was her reply:

Hey hon,

No need to thank me, you did all of this yourself. He's definitely your soulmate, no doubts. You deserve this. I'm so happy for you.

Sue xx

I am incredibly grateful the universe whispered in my ear.

Elise xx

.

11

Purpose

18th November 2021

Dear Universe,

I feel like I finally have answers. My youngest daughter received a diagnosis of autism today. I know lots of parents in this situation are in denial and don't want to hear it, but strangely, I feel this sense of relief. Now we have an understanding of how and why her outlook on this world is different to what society says it should be. The profound thing about her diagnosis today is not that it's unexpected or unwelcome, as I knew she was likely on the spectrum from the time she was a little baby, but that her diagnosis would provide me with some answers about myself. I get her. I understand her. I feel her anxieties as much as she does mine. I understand how exhausting it is to mask and protect ourselves from the world and its expectations. I know what it's like to work so hard to hide your intelligence from others in order to fit in and not stand out. I know what it's like to remember facts and figures and be an encyclopedia of knowledge on uncool topics. I know what it's like to smile on the outside but be screaming on the inside from worries and anxieties. I know what it's like to have a brain that just won't switch off. I know what it's like to be too honest and naive about everything and only look for the good in people. I know what it's like to care too much, to feel too much and to have so much creativity, empathy and compassion you don't know what to do with it. I know what it is like to overthink everything, to overanalyse and go over things in your head again and again.

Crowded places, germs, large social gatherings, loud noises, disorganisation and people's insincerity are all triggers for me as much as they are for her. For all of these years, I've worried I have made her like this, and I've rubbed my own anxieties and traits off on her. I've blamed myself, just like her father has always blamed me for everything. But why is my other gorgeous daughter that I raised exactly the same, so different? Why haven't I caused this in *her*? As I sat quietly in the paediatrician's office processing what all of this meant, he smiled at me as though he knew what I was thinking. He put his arm on my shoulder and said, "Considering that Autism Spectrum Disorder is predominantly in the genes, have you ever considered that you are in fact on the spectrum yourself?"

I couldn't believe he would say such a thing. I'm not autistic. I have never had tantrums or meltdowns and I was a straight A student at school. I was Head Girl! I never caused trouble or was a behaviour problem. I always followed rules. I always did the right thing. I strived for perfectionism in everything that I attempted. I loved routine, I loved school, I loved endless learning. I loved talking. I loved facts. I loved order and cleanliness and germs were and still are my enemy! I loved keeping my brain busy. I didn't like being pushed out of my comfort zone or plans changing, and I was never a rule breaker. I was good at all subjects, and I could do anything I put my mind to. I got along with teachers better than students because I felt they were more on my level and understood me better. I had maturity beyond my years and always felt different to my peers. As a child, I already saw the world from an adult perspective. Maybe I have been masking for all of those years? Autism does present differently in everyone.

I sat there in shock, not knowing what to say. It wasn't until I had a little time to process what this kind doctor was asking me that I realised how profound my daughter's diagnosis was for me as much as it is for her.

"Autism isn't always what society perceives it to be," the doctor continued. "It can be a gift. Some of the most intelligent, kindest, and most creative souls I have ever met are on the spectrum."

How could he tell from just talking to me? How did he know? It must be the years of expertise in his field and my oversharing nature that created the flashing lights. I agreed with him. I think I am on the spectrum. I do have a neurodivergent brain, and I am comfortable with that. I feel a huge sense of relief. It is like a huge weight has lifted off my shoulders. I don't feel like I even need to seek a diagnosis for myself; I don't need the label, because I understand who I am. I am at peace with all of it, because finally I understand.

Elise xx

21st December 2021

Dear Universe,

My name is Elise. I am 41 years old. I love the beach
and swimming, and water is still my happy place. The
beach is medicine for my soul and creativity runs
through my veins. Writing, painting, drawing and
creating is what keeps my spark dancing in the breeze.
I loved school and learning so much that I chose to
become a teacher, so I could share my love for
learning. I am an overly sensitive soul and I pride
myself on my kind and caring nature. I am
oversensitive and feel things deeply due to my
neurodivergent brain that absorbs everything around
me. I married my first boyfriend because I felt that no
one else in this world would ever love me. The years
of bullying at my first high school destroyed my self-
belief and confidence so much that I felt I didn't
deserve any better. I felt I didn't deserve to be loved.
My best friend is still Hannah and even though life
hasn't treated either of us kindly due to a plethora of
health conditions, our friendship has always been kind.
It is funny how some friendships seem to last a lifetime
and others are a fleeting meeting, yet each has its
special purpose. It is often not until after someone

leaves our life that we recognise the significance of their connection to our path. It is strange how our acquaintances with people throughout life become a network of webs and it often isn't until later we recognise the links to the past and the purpose or meaning of that connection.

I have been writing to you, Universe, for all of those years but I didn't think you were listening. I realise now that it was me that was not taking notice of the signs you put before me. Sometimes I didn't want to see them because they weren't always what I wanted to hear, see or believe. I didn't want to trust my gut instincts because what my gut was telling me might make my life too difficult, too imperfect.

So, what would I tell my sixteen-year-old self all those years ago when I started writing to the universe? What words of wisdom could I give that self-conscious teenager with the world at her feet?

There is no perfect life, there is no perfect destination we must reach. It is not about the destination, but the journey. What we take from this journey called life is up to us. We can choose to ignore the opportunities along our path, or we can choose to push ourselves out of our comfort zone and learn and grow along the way. Sometimes our decisions are going to be the right ones, when we listen to and follow the signs from the universe, but sometimes we will make mistakes. Sometimes we will make bad choices that will take us on a detour through the back streets in places we don't want to visit. In life, there is no turning back or reversing, however we can look back upon our journey and reflect. Mistakes are okay, they are opportunities for growth and learning and a chance to send what we want, desire and deserve out into the universe.

What you put out into the universe will come back to you, even if it takes time. The energy you exude attracts the same, like a mirror. Accept the things you cannot change and focus on the things you can, and want, to transform. Connect with life and people in the present moment. Be kind. Kindness is the greatest virtue.

Life is short. Time is much more precious than money, so spend it wisely. The years creep along quickly, spend them with people that deserve your energy and give energy to things that you love doing. Forgiveness allows you to move forward to the future, unforgiveness holds you backwards in the past.

Forgiveness is not forgetting, but remembering your worth and letting go of anger, bitterness and resentment that erodes us away like the tide.

For too many years I have sought perfection and wasted time focusing on the past or the future, instead of living in the present. My failed marriage gave me two beautiful children. I realise now that the universe put people on my path for a reason; to learn to love myself and to finally believe in myself once again. After all that I have endured, the universe wanted me to see myself through the eyes of others who valued my worth.

I have helped people find their way in this world, as others have helped me find mine. When I finally learned to love and appreciate myself, my soulmate, the love of my life, appeared on my path. Someone who deserves my love as much as I deserve theirs. True love is worth the wait. True love will come knocking on your door when you least expect it. Nothing will be forced, it will just happen naturally. True love might present itself through an old friend, a chance meeting, or an online date. But true love only happens when one loves and accepts themselves. The universe knows when you are ready.

Dear Universe, thanks to you delivering things along my journey - even though it took me way too long to realise - not only did I find true love, but I finally understand the meaning of life. Yes, the meaning of life is to love, but one can only love others when first they learn to love themselves.

We all have light and energy inside of us, but sometimes that light dims, and we need others to help spark the flame to glow once again. Love, joy, peace and happiness is that light within all of us. Each of us has a different fuel that keeps that light luminescent. Each of us have different passions and dreams. Each of us has a different purpose in life. The trickiest part is discovering what your purpose is. Put your energy into discovering your passions and finding your purpose in this world.

This beam of illumination that lights us up from within is not something to be found by searching the universe. It is only something we can find by searching within ourselves, the true purpose that drives our soul our own purpose in this infinite universe. I have finally found my purpose, which has always been to help others. I want to help others by sharing my letters to the universe. This is my story, my journey. So, what is the power of the universe? What is the purpose to life? To love and be loved of course! For a life without love is an empty one. Love is the most powerful energy in the universe, which starts with the power of love and belief in oneself.

Elise xx

THE END